YOU CHOOSE
BOOKS

D0537842

Little Red Riding Hood

AN INTERACTIVE FAIRY TALE ADVENTURE

by Eric Braun

illustrated by
Mariano Epelbaum

raintree
a Capstone company — publishers for children

Raintree is an imprint of Capstone Global Library Limited, a company incorporated in England and Wales having its registered office at 7 Pilgrim Street, London, EC4V 6LB – Registered company number: 6695582

www.raintree.co.uk
myorders@raintree.co.uk

Edited by Kristen Mohn
Designed by Ted Williams
Creative Director: Nathan Gassman
Production by Tori Abraham

ISBN 978 1 4747 0716 9
19 18 17 16 15
10 9 8 7 6 5 4 3 2 1

British Library Cataloguing in Publication Data
A full catalogue record for this book is available from the British Library

Acknowledgements
Shutterstock: solarbird, background

Printed in China.

Contents

About your adventure 4

CHAPTER 1
Alone in the woods 7

CHAPTER 2
Bad reputation 11

CHAPTER 3
Fleeing through the night 53

CHAPTER 4
Attack plans 83

CHAPTER 5
A little bit of
history about Little Red 107

Comprehension questions 111
Books 112
Website 112

The woods are dark and deep. And they're easy to get lost in. Even worse, you sense there's something out there that means you harm.

In this fairy tale, you control your fate. Put on the cape of Little Red Riding Hood and make choices to determine what happens next.

Chapter One sets the scene. Then you choose which path to take. Follow the directions as you read the stories. The decisions you make will change the outcome of your adventure. When you've finished one path, go back and read the others for new perspectives and more adventures ... if you make it out of the woods.

Alone in the woods

You are walking alone through a forest in the dark of night. A picnic basket trembles in your hand. You move quickly along the path, careful to avoid rocks and tree roots that seem to grab at your feet. The forest itself feels alive.

With one eye you scan the dark shadows between the trees. What moved in there? Was that a pair of eyes?

Where you come from, everyone is afraid of these woods – and so are you.

People say that children disappear in here. They say watch out for wolves in this forest – the wolves will try to trick you, scare you, take you. They say to never go into these woods alone, and never, ever go in at night.

Yet here you are. You wouldn't be if it wasn't so important. You must get to grandmother. Everything depends on it.

After walking for some time, nothing bad happens, and you begin to relax. The stars are out. The owls hoot. It's not so scary, you think. It's actually quite nice.

That's when you hear the voice: "Where are you going, child?"

TO BE A MODERN-DAY CHILD WALKING THROUGH A LARGE CITY PARK, TURN TO PAGE II.

TO BE A CHILD CAUGHT IN A TERRIBLE WAR, TURN TO PAGE 53.

TO BE A FUTURISTIC AGENT WORKING AGAINST AN EVIL CORPORATION, TURN TO PAGE 83.

CHAPTER 2

Bad reputation

The Fairy Tale wolves are angry. Lately, nice wolves have made news headlines for helping old ladies cross the street, volunteering at the children's hospital and donating money to build new playgrounds. One wolf has even pledged to run around City Park 1,000 times to raise awareness for homeless people. The news channels have all been covering that story!

The wolves from "Peter and the Wolf", "The Boy Who Cried Wolf", "The Three Little Pigs" and "Little Red Riding Hood" have retired to the city to relax – but not to stop being bad. They can't stand by and watch these nice wolves ruin their hard-earned reputation for evil-doing.

To restore their bad name, they have teamed up to terrorize citizens who go into the park at night. You have heard the tortured screams of the poor fools who got caught in the park after dark.

Now you are one of those poor fools.

Here's how it happened: Your grandmother became unwell and asked you to bring her some milk and Yummy-Pops cereal – her favourite food – to cheer her up. You love spending time with her. The two of you watch funny cat videos, knit hilarious finger puppets and eat bowl after bowl of cereal. You especially love the stories of her brave adventures sailing a stormy ocean, climbing a towering mountain and outwitting burglars. She even survived an encounter with three bears when she was a girl.

Unfortunately, she lives on the other side of the park. Even though the park is scary, you couldn't say no to grandmother. The park stretches for miles. Going around it takes hours. Better to just run through it quickly and get it over with. Anyway, you need to toughen up, like Gran.

But now that a wolf is standing in front of you, you wish you had at least waited until morning. He leans against a lamp post and uses a gleaming white fang to clean out the mud (or is it blood?) from underneath one of his long, sharp claws. A silver stripe of fur runs from his nose to his tail.

With a trembling hand, you remove your ear phones. "What did you say?"

"Where are you going, child?"

TO MAKE A RUN FOR IT, TURN TO PAGE 14.

TO TRY TO TALK YOUR WAY OUT OF THIS, TURN TO PAGE 16.

You run towards the gated entrance to the park, not far ahead. Surely the wolf won't chase you into the well-lit street.

"What do you fear?" the wolf says behind you. Right behind you. In your ear. He's quick.

Panting to catch your breath, you turn and look into his yellow eyes. Gran wouldn't be afraid, and it angers you that you're being a chicken. You remember the news reports. Maybe this is one of those good wolves. "I'm not afraid," you say.

The wolf's lips stretch back into a wide, toothy grin. "Of course," he purrs. "But you should be afraid. This park is full of bad wolves. We good wolves can only do so much to protect people. You shouldn't be here alone."

"You're a good wolf?" you ask, your voice trembling.

"Child," the wolf says, "if I were a big bad wolf, would you not be eaten up by now?"

He makes a good point. But still, something about this wolf makes the hairs on the back of your neck stand up. You pull up your hood and say, "Well, I'd better go."

"Better come with me," he says. "I'll keep you safe … from the bad wolves."

TO FOLLOW THE WOLF, TURN TO PAGE 19.

TO LEAVE HIM, TURN TO PAGE 22.

"I am going to visit my grandmother," you say to Stripe, the wolf. "I'm late, so if you don't mind, I'll be going now."

Stripe lets out a low growl. "I do mind," he says. "You don't get to come through this park at night without paying a price." He cleans another claw on his fang and scrapes it along the lamp post to sharpen it. You've seen similar claw marks around the park, like graffiti.

"W-w-what price?" you ask.

Stripe reaches a hairy arm towards you, and his claws gleam in the lamplight. Saliva drips from his open jaws. You back away.

"Wait!" you say, thinking fast. "I know how you can get rid of all those nice wolves. Those goody-two-shoes wolves deserve to be punished!" you yell, slamming your fist into your hand.

Stripe lowers his paw. "Keep talking, child," he says.

You look both ways as if about to tell a huge secret. "I know where wolfsbane grows," you say quietly. "I just have to drop off this cereal with my grandmother first, and then I'll meet you back here."

17

TURN THE PAGE.

The wolf's eyes bulge out of their sockets. "Do you know how many good wolves I can kill with a poison like that?" he asks excitedly. But then his eyes narrow again. "How do I know you'll come back?" he says.

"We'll exchange mobile phone numbers," you say, pulling out your phone. You're not sure if the wolf believes your story.

TO RUN FOR IT, TURN TO PAGE 23.

TO EXCHANGE MOBILE PHONE NUMBERS, TURN TO PAGE 24.

"OK, thanks," you say. If the evil wolves are even creepier than this wolf, you don't want to meet them.

"Excellent," the wolf purrs, taking you by the hand with his hairy paw. He leads you off the path into the trees. The yellow eyes of other wolves glow in the darkness. Something inside your head starts to wail like a siren. This was a mistake! You try to wrench your hand away, but the wolf holds tight.

"Let me go!" you scream.

"Yes, let the child go!" says a hoarse voice. You twist around to see another wolf loping towards you – a good wolf!

TURN THE PAGE.

You feel the striped wolf release your hand.
"Run!" the good wolf yells. You scramble to
your feet and sprint towards the park gates. You
hear the terrible, snarling sounds of the two
wolves fighting.

You leave the park and run quickly to grandmother's flat. As you approach the building, you see a man with a badge carrying a rifle coming towards the park. He's one of the new "wolf patrolmen" who have been working to protect people from the bad wolves. As you stop to tell him what happened, you think you see a wolf creeping in the shadows on the street.

The patrolman runs into the park to investigate. You push the button for your grandmother's flat, and a scratchy voice croaks through the speaker: "Who is it?"

Gran sounds really ill! "Little Red," you say, and she buzzes you up. When you get to her flat, the door is slightly ajar. That's unusual – she always keeps it locked.

TO PEEK INSIDE, TURN TO PAGE 26.

TO WALK IN, TURN TO PAGE 28.

You begin to walk away but the wolf steps in front of you. "You're not going anywhere," he says.

Just as you suspected: He's an evil Fairy Tale wolf – not one of the good wolves. Your only hope is to distract him. "Look!" you say, pointing into the trees. "That nice wolf is picking up litter in the park!"

"What?" the wolf says, following your gaze. "I hate those good wolves!"

While he's looking away, you turn and sprint towards the park gates. You throw the picnic basket back at the wolf, who is now hot on your heels. He's so close you can smell his breath.

Just outside the gate, you see the shadow of a tall man with a rifle.

TO CALL OUT FOR HELP, TURN TO PAGE 30.

TO KEEP RUNNING, TURN TO PAGE 32.

22

You wait for the wolf to put his hand into his own pocket to fish out his phone. When he does, you turn and bolt for the park gate.

You hear the wolf's phone thunk to the ground and the swift patter of his paws as he comes after you. You hear his breathing – or is that your breathing? You soon realize you're hearing the panting of an entire pack of wolves. The Fairy Tale wolves have teamed up to share in the pleasure of gobbling you up.

You wish you really did have some wolfsbane.

THE END

TO FOLLOW ANOTHER PATH, TURN TO PAGE 9.

You tell the wolf a made-up mobile number. You feel your temples drip with sweat, but you try to act naturally. The wolf watches as you attempt to casually walk away. When you reach the edge of the park, you run out onto a bustling city street with relief.

Near the entrance to your grandmother's block of flats, a man wearing a badge holds a rifle to his shoulder. He winks at you as you enter the building. You don't recognize him.

You press the button for your grandmother's flat, but there's no reply. You press it again. Finally Gran's scratchy voice comes over the intercom. "Who is it?"

"It's me, Gran."

She buzzes open the door, and you walk upstairs to her second-floor flat. You find the bedroom door open with your grandmother lying in bed. The blankets are pulled up over her head.

You sniff the air. What is that smell? After a second, you recognize it: Stripe. He's here somewhere.

TO STAY IN THE DOORWAY FOR A QUICK ESCAPE, TURN TO PAGE 33.

TO GO IN TO SEE YOUR GRANDMOTHER, TURN TO PAGE 37.

You peek inside and see "Stripe", the wolf. He's
slinking in through an open window and across
the floor towards your grandmother's bed! As
you're watching, he lifts her up with his meaty
paws and devours her in one bite. It happens so
quickly, you don't even have time to scream.

Stripe, still swallowing the massive, fighting lump of your grandmother, turns and sees you. He gulps, saliva dripping off his hairy chin. You can't believe he's still hungry, but he's looking at you with a gleam in his eye that tells you he is.

Stripe burps and picks one of your grandmother's slippers out from between his teeth. "Come, child," he growls.

You look around. You can't see anything that could be used as a weapon except perhaps your grandmother's walking frame – you could whack him with it.

27

Maybe you should run down the stairs. Stripe is full and fat, now. He might not be able to catch you. You think: What would Gran do?

TO RUN AWAY, TURN TO PAGE 39.

TO FIGHT THE WOLF, TURN TO PAGE 42.

You walk in. There in the living room is Stripe the wolf, snarling at your grandmother. When he sees you, he says, "Excellent, now I can eat you both."

"Not if we can help it," Gran says, taking advantage of the distraction you made.

Stripe leaps towards her, but in a surprising blur, she whacks him across the muzzle with something. She smiles and holds up the cricket bat from her days on the first women's team.

"Good hit, Gran!" you say as Stripe flops to the floor.

But then he gets back up, his own blood staining his lips. As Stripe slinks towards Gran, he shoves you to the floor and you bang your head on the fireplace. You watch as Gran swings the bat again, but this time Stripe is ready. He catches the bat in his great mouth and crunches down, splintering the wood. You and Gran exchange a horrified look.

Gums bleeding and full of splinters, Stripe turns on Gran. This time, it looks like he's going in for the kill. You don't know what to do.

TO MAKE ONE LAST ATTACK ON THE WOLF, TURN TO PAGE 45.

TO PLAY DEAD AND HOPE HE LEAVES YOU ALONE, TURN TO PAGE 47.

29

"Help!" you yell. The man lifts his rifle to his shoulder and points it behind you, but then he lowers it again. You realize the footsteps behind you have stopped. You reach the man and stop to rest, panting.

You look back into the park, but the wolf is nowhere to be seen.

"Thank you," you say. "You scared him away. He was going to..." But the man runs off without a word. Is he pursuing the wolf? You don't hang around to find out. You hurry across the busy street to your grandmother's block of flats and press the button for her flat. She buzzes you in.

You find her lying in bed with the covers over her head. She must really be ill.

"I'm sorry, Gran," you call into the room.
"I lost the cereal. I threw it at a wolf that was chasing me."

"It's okay, dear," she says weakly. "I really just wanted to see you."

Just then there's a loud knock at the door. A deep voice says, "Open up – quick!"

Your grandmother struggles to sit up in bed. "Let him in!" she says.

TO OPEN THE DOOR, TURN TO PAGE 48.

TO FIND OUT WHO IT IS FIRST, TURN TO PAGE 50.

You run harder towards the gate, gasping for breath. The wolf's bounding steps close in behind you.

Just as you're about to escape, you feel sharp claws dig into your shoulders. You crumple to the ground. You hear a piercing howl and realize that it's coming from you.

Your shredded back and shoulders ignite with pain. The wolf's saliva drips into your ear, and his knife-like teeth sink into your neck. You hear a rifle shot and the yelp of the wolf as he's hit. Then you feel the weight of him collapse upon you.

The man with the rifle rushes up to you, but the look on his face tells you there's no hope. Your howl turns into a moan, and then everything is silent.

THE END

TO FOLLOW ANOTHER PATH, TURN TO PAGE 9.

"Gran," you call from the doorway. "Are you okay?"

"I'm okay," she calls back. "One of those kind wolves was here delivering my shopping. Can you smell him?"

You relax. "So that's what I can smell," you say. You walk into her bedroom. But lying there in her dark bedroom, she doesn't look right. "Gran," you say, "what big eyes you've got."

"Yes, dear," she replies. "The better to see you with."

You step closer and see her hand on top of the blanket. "And what large hands you've got." **33**

"The better to hug you with."

TURN THE PAGE.

"My goodness, Gran, what big, hairy ears you've got."

"The better to hear your sweet voice, my dear." She smiles, showing all her teeth.

"And what big teeth…" you whisper.

"Those," grandmother says, lowering the blanket and setting foot – or paw – to the floor, "are all the better to eat you with!"

You run out of the bedroom just as the man carrying the rifle bursts in. You cower on the floor and hear a loud bang. When you open your eyes, you see Stripe lying dead on the floor.

The man grabs a long knife from the kitchen and slices open the wolf's stomach. He reaches into the bloody guts and pulls Gran out by the wrists. She comes up gasping for air.

TURN THE PAGE.

While your grandmother takes a bath, you talk to the man over bowls of Yummy-Pops. He's a Wolf Watch officer – part of a non-profit organization set up to protect citizens from bad wolves. "I saw you come out of the park," he says. "I knew there would be a wolf following you."

"Thank goodness you saw me," you say.

"Now," the man says. "Do you want to know where the wolfsbane really is?"

You nod. No more wolves will push you around.

36

THE END

TO FOLLOW ANOTHER PATH, TURN TO PAGE 9.

As soon as you walk in, you realize something is wrong – very wrong. Your grandmother is nowhere to be seen, but Stripe is standing by the bed putting on her pyjamas.

"What are you doing?" you say.

"Digesting a nice dinner," the wolf says calmly.

"Where's Gran?"

"I knew that phone number you gave me was fake, so I followed you here. While you were waiting downstairs, I climbed up the fire escape."

"Where's Gran?" you repeat.

"Such a lovely woman," Stripe says. "And so delicious."

TURN THE PAGE.

You turn to run, but the wolf is quicker. With both paws he lifts you high over his gaping mouth, then lowers you headfirst down his throat. The saliva coats you, and his slimy throat muscles contract and pull your head down as he shoves your legs deeper into his mouth with his fists.

You throw elbows and try to kick, but you can't move. It's like being in an extremely tight, slippery sleeping bag. You can't breathe. Just as you are about to faint, you feel a wrinkly hand grab hold of yours. At least you and Gran will be together.

38

THE END

TO FOLLOW ANOTHER PATH, TURN TO PAGE 9.

There's no way you can fight a wolf – you're just a child! You remember the patrolman. You turn and race down the stairs, two at a time. Stripe's snarls echo in the stairwell behind you.

When you reach the street, you see the patrolman with two good wolves. Stripe barges out of the door behind you. You start to duck in case any shots are fired, but then you stop. "Don't shoot him in the stomach! He ate my grandmother!" you call out.

Stripe dives on the patrolman, knocking the rifle from his hands. The other two wolves try to pull him off, but Stripe bucks them away. The four of them fight for a few minutes, grunts and blood everywhere. Eventually the man rolls out from under the pack and takes aim at Stripe. He pulls the trigger, but it only clicks.

TURN THE PAGE.

Stripe springs to his hind legs and gives the patrolman a mighty shove in the chest with both paws. The man falls backwards over a car and lands with a sickening thud.

Stripe wipes blood from his lips. "Look at you two!" he says to the other wolves, who are cowering injured on the ground. "You should be ashamed! That man would have killed you. But you helped him! You go around shovelling snow for senior citizens and giving sweets to children. YOU ARE WOLVES! Act like it!"

All three wolves are breathing hard and bleeding. The two "good" wolves look at you with a glint in their eyes.

"Show some self-respect," Stripe says. He rubs his stomach. "I've got a belly full of grandmother, and it feels great! You should try it." The other two wolves narrow their eyes at you. Then all three approach. It's only a question of which will get to you first.

THE END

TO FOLLOW ANOTHER PATH, TURN TO PAGE 9.

Gran always did the courageous thing. You
know that she will fight. You run towards her
armchair, grab her metal walking frame and lift it
over your head. Then you bring it down hard on
Stripe's muzzle.

"Ooof!" the wolf says, staggering.

Encouraged, you do it again, but the second hit doesn't seem to hurt him as much. Stripe looks up at you and laughs.

"You'll be a tasty morsel," Stripe says, covering you with his terrible breath.

You raise the walking frame again, but while it's above your head, Stripe lunges. He slashes you across the belly with his razor-sharp claws. Your red hoodie is shredded, and blood seeps into the fabric. Stripe slashes again but you hook his paw in the walking frame. You twist, turning his paw at a painful angle. Stripe yowls in pain and looks up at you with big, bulging eyes. "My, what big eyes you have," you whisper to him as you push him backwards right out of the window and onto the pavement far below.

43

TURN THE PAGE.

You get a big knife from the kitchen, run down to the street, and cut open the wolf's belly. Your grandmother crawls out. She coughs and spits, and after a few seconds she stands up and hugs you.

"He said he was a good wolf here with my milk delivery," she says, shaking her head. Then she whispers in your ear, "Thank you. This will be one to tell *your* grandchildren."

THE END

TO FOLLOW ANOTHER PATH, TURN TO PAGE 9.

44

You have no weapons, but you can't give up when your grandmother is about to be eaten. You grope around for anything to hit Stripe with and find a cushion. You swat the wolf with it. *Thwap!*

Stripe looks at you in disbelief, then blinks a couple of times as puffs of dust surround him. Suddenly a massive sneeze storms from his maw. Saliva, snot and a little blood spew out. Again, you whack Stripe with the cushion. More dust puffs into his face.

"Stop it!" he says, rubbing his nose and sneezing some more.

45

You keep hitting him. Dust floats in the air like fog. Wow, Gran really doesn't clean very often! Stripe collapses to the floor in a sneezing fit. He blows his nose on a rug, tears running down his face.

TURN THE PAGE.

You lunge for the walking frame. You lift it high, then bring it down hard on Stripe's head. The sneezing stops for good.

You rush over to check Gran's pulse. It is weak, but she's alive. You call 999. The paramedics who arrive are good wolves who have devoted their lives to helping others.

"Put her on the platter," one of them says, as they pick her up. "I mean the stretcher," he corrects himself, looking at you nervously.

"Are you sure you're good wolves?" you ask.

46 "Old habits die hard," the wolf says.

THE END

TO FOLLOW ANOTHER PATH, TURN TO PAGE 9.

Your only hope is to play dead. You lay as still as possible, barely breathing, as Stripe tears into your grandmother. You are forced to listen to her shrieks and "ows!" along with the wolf's rude chewing sounds as you wait.

Finally you hear him burp and sigh. Then his claws click across the floor towards you. You realize you were a fool to think he'd leave you alone. You should have at least tried to fight. Instead, you're going to be dessert.

THE END

TO FOLLOW ANOTHER PATH, TURN TO PAGE 9.

You open the door to the tall man with the rifle. "It's you," you say. He pushes in, then shuts and bolts the door.

"Hello, Albert," Gran croaks.

"Hello, Granny," he says. "I just got a call from the three little pigs, and they say the wolves are huffing and puffing again. That brick house is going down tonight unless we do something. I was hoping you could help."

"I just don't have the energy for a fight tonight. But perhaps my granddaughter can help?"

"M-m-me?" you stammer. "I just got away from the wolves, I'm not going back out there!" But you don't want to let down Gran so you agree to help. Albert puts a rifle in your trembling hands and leads you to the brick house of the pigs. There you see several wolves huffing and puffing in unison. The house buckles under the gales but holds.

You and Albert raise your rifles and shoot at the same time. Two of the wolves drop dead, and the other two run. The house is safe.

"Thank you!" one of the pigs yells, waving a hoof. You feel exhilarated! You realize that you might have a bit of your grandmother's courage in you after all.

THE END

TO FOLLOW ANOTHER PATH, TURN TO PAGE 9.

What if it's the wolf? Better to be safe. You pick up Gran's lucky cricket bat and call out, "Who's there?"

"It's Albert. Let me in!" the voice says.

"How can we be sure it's you?" you ask.

"Oh, no!" he yells.

"What?" you yell back.

"Let him in, child!" Gran says desperately.

You open the door a crack and peer out to see the man with the badge from the park firing his rifle down the stairs. A wolf on the stairs collapses, but two others approach.

The man tries to reload his gun, but one of the wolves leaps up the stairs and pounces on him. You slam the door and lock it. Screams, growls and howls come through the shaking walls.

"Was it Albert?" Gran says. "The man with the rifle? He is coming to help us get rid of the wolves."

You lean against the door, realizing your hesitation cost Albert his life. Even worse, the wolves will be bursting into Gran's flat at any moment.

THE END

TO FOLLOW ANOTHER PATH, TURN TO PAGE 9.

CHAPTER 3

Fleeing through the night

You have never seen your parents so scared. They dragged you out of bed in the middle of the night, gave you a small basket of food and brought you to this path at the edge of the woods. Wanting to stay hidden, they don't light a lantern. It is very dark.

"They are coming," your father says. You know who he means: the Soldiers. They are coming to take the children away. You, your family, your friends and everyone in your village have been worrying about this for weeks.

53

"Walk quickly along this path," your father says, "and do not stop until you reach the village on the far side of the forest. If you walk quickly, you will arrive by mid-morning tomorrow. The town is called Bon Jardin."

He tells you that when you reach the town, a kind, grandmotherly woman called Simone will be waiting for you in the first small cottage you come to. She will feed you and hide you from the Soldiers. She has hidden many children. You can trust Simone – and only Simone. "Avoid anyone else," your father says. "If anyone stops you, tell them that you are taking a cake to your poorly grandmother."

You hug your father and mother, who is weeping softly. "When will I see you?" you ask.

"Soon," your mother promises. But she doesn't sound very sure. How can she be? Nobody can predict what will happen during war.

"Hurry now," your father says. You do as you are told and run into the woods with only faint starlight to guide you.

For several hours you are alone and your fears settle. But suddenly a twig snaps in the trees, and you freeze. A deep voice asks, "Where are you going, child?" A Soldier steps out of the woods.

TO RUN AWAY FROM HIM ALONG THE PATH, TURN TO PAGE 56.

TO TELL HIM THAT YOU'RE TAKING A CAKE TO YOUR GRANDMOTHER, TURN TO PAGE 58.

You're small and fast. You think you can lose him, so you run.

"Stop!" he says. "Or the penalty will be severe!"

It will be severe if I *do* stop, you think. He runs after you and a beam of light sweeps across the path. You're faster than he is and soon you're able to gain some distance. But you're getting tired.

"Stop!" he yells again – his voice is far away. He fires his gun, and a flash of fear comes over you. You believe he will shoot you if he catches you.

He is not going to give up. You think he might track you all the way to Simone's cottage, which would be a disaster. You can't put all those other hidden children at risk. Even if he catches you, at least the rest will be safe. You dart off the path and into a thicket to hide.

After what must be an hour or more, you no longer hear the Soldier. Your face is pocked with insect bites, and you gently raise your hand to scratch. It's the first time you have moved even a centimetre in a long time.

TO STAY HIDDEN FOR A BIT LONGER, TURN TO PAGE 61.

TO QUIETLY GET BACK ON THE PATH AND KEEP GOING, TURN TO PAGE 62.

You stop, and the Soldier steps into your path. The sleeves of his uniform are rolled up, revealing very hairy arms. He licks the lips of his large, wolfish grin.

"Where are you going?" he asks again.

"Just to my grandmother's house," you reply. "She is ill and I'm taking her some cake to cheer her up."

The Soldier strokes his long beard. Then he says, "And where does your grandmother live?"

You step away. The Soldier steps closer. He

draws his pistol.

"Tell me where she lives," he says, "or I will shoot you. And don't lie, child. I can tell when children lie."

The way he looks at you with those big, yellow eyes, you wouldn't be surprised if he *can* tell when children lie. Soldiers are well-trained interrogators. Perhaps you can tell him a partial truth and run ahead to Bon Jardin to warn Simone. At least then you'd have a chance of surviving.

TO LIE AND GIVE HIM A FALSE LOCATION, TURN TO PAGE 63.

TO TELL HIM A PARTIAL TRUTH ABOUT THE TOWN OF BON JARDIN, TURN TO PAGE 64.

You rest your head on your knees. Soon you hear footsteps coming. You were right to stay hidden! As he approaches, your fear increases and you struggle to calm your breathing. A badger stumbles through the thicket near you, and the Soldier shines his light in your direction. When he sees the badger, he sweeps the light back towards the path. That was close.

But he doesn't keep walking. He stands on the path listening. Or is he smelling the air? He gazes all around as if he can sense that you are near. A bat swoops across the path.

You realize that your red cape and hood are bright – easy to see if the light hits them. For a moment the Soldier turns away from you to look down the path towards your home village.

TO REMOVE THE CAPE AND HOOD AND STAY HIDDEN, TURN TO PAGE 66.

TO GET UP AND RUN, TURN TO PAGE 68.

You step gingerly out of the thicket, carefully avoiding any twigs that might snap underfoot. You crouch low for a few seconds, but you don't sense any movement. Perhaps he's really gone.

You start back on the path towards Bon Jardin, only now you are running. You've been hiding a long time, and dawn will come soon. As you run, your breathing echoes in your head, and your own footsteps begin to sound very loud. Your mind is playing tricks on you.

You stop and listen. You can't be sure, but you think you hear the Soldier some distance behind you. Better keep running – you can't waste any more time hiding or you'll be caught in the daylight.

TURN TO PAGE 68.

You'd rather risk lying than put Simone and the other children in danger. "She lives in the town," you say, pointing back towards your own village. "I was just picking some berries for her."

The Soldier reaches down and lifts you by your red hood. Your feet dangle in the air. His breath smells like a dead animal. He holds his pistol in front of you.

"You shouldn't have tested me," he says and knocks you on the head with his pistol. When you wake up, your hands are tied together and he is dragging you by the hood along the path. You don't know what will happen to you, but you know it won't be good. You try to take comfort in the fact that you didn't put Simone and the other children at risk. At least they still have a chance.

THE END

TO FOLLOW ANOTHER PATH, TURN TO PAGE 9.

"She lives in Bon Jardin," you say.

"Strange time to be visiting," the Soldier says.

"She's very ill," you say. "She's all alone. I was worried."

"Where in Bon Jardin does she live?"

"She runs an inn on the main road," you lie.

"Very well," he says and lets go of your hood. You step away from him. When he doesn't follow, you turn to run down the path.

After more than two hours, you arrive in the village, sweating and exhausted. You see the cottage, just as father described. Two large brown lorries are parked near by. As you approach the door to the cottage, you hear voices inside arguing. A woman is sobbing.

Down the road you see Soldiers escorting a line of children from a school. Despair fills your heart. The Soldiers found them. It's all your fault. In worrying about your own safety, you betrayed a whole village and the hundreds of children hidden here.

You turn to find a Soldier standing behind you. He orders you to join the other children being loaded onto the lorries.

THE END

TO FOLLOW ANOTHER PATH, TURN TO PAGE 9.

Carefully you untie the string at your throat.
You pull the hood and cape off slowly. As you lean
onto your side to hide the garment under your legs,
you put your hand on a thorny branch. Before you
can think, you cry out – a short yelp of pain.

The Soldier turns and shines his lantern in your
direction. You remain perfectly still.

The Soldier steps closer to you. "Come out,
child," he says.

You hold your breath.

"Show yourself, now!" he barks.

Your heart thumps and your hands tremble.
Suddenly the light form his lantern is in your eyes,
and you're blinded. Branches and bracken crack as
he tramples towards you. The light gets brighter,
suddenly recedes, and then comes flashing back
as he brings the lantern down on your head with
a clunk.

You come round with a horrible headache.
You groan and roll over. "Get up," the Soldier says.

He ties your hands and leads you stumbling
back towards your own village. He takes you to
the train station and loads you into a big carriage
with lots of other children. You're so scared you
throw up. You have heard of these train carriages.
Children taken away on them do not come back.
All around you, people are crying. A boy you
know is calling out the names of his sisters and
brothers, but no one is answering.

You close your eyes and cry too.

THE END

TO FOLLOW ANOTHER PATH, TURN TO PAGE 9.

You've never run so fast or so far in your life. You keep running until you emerge from the woods, exhausted. It's morning – the sky is blue and birds chirp in the trees. Up ahead you see a small house. It must be Simone's cottage. Further along the street you see a church, a school and more houses.

You hurry to the cottage and knock.

"Come in," says a gruff voice from inside.

It doesn't sound like a woman's voice, but you open the door and lean your head in. At first you don't see anyone. From another room comes the voice again. "Come in here, child."

Things don't seem right, so before going in you grab the shovel that is leaning near the door. Your whole body is on edge. From the bedroom come the sounds of furniture sliding on the floor and then a loud thud.

"Run!" a woman's voice screams. You hear
someone being hit hard, and then the Soldier
comes out of the room.

TO RUN OUT OF THE DOOR, TURN TO PAGE 70.

TO TRY TO SAVE SIMONE, TURN TO PAGE 72.

You drop the shovel and run from the
cottage with the Soldier chasing after you. You
leap down the porch steps and nearly run into
a tall man with a long robe and beard – and a
rifle aimed right at you.

Bang!

You collapse to the ground and cover your
ears. When you look up, you see the Soldier
lying dead behind you, blood trickling from a
hole in his chest.

"Come with me," says the man with the rifle.
"I said come on!" he shouts, grabbing your arm.

The man is a reverend. He takes you back
into Simone's cottage where she is tied up in the
bedroom. He frees her and then says, "Get the
child into hiding, quickly."

While the reverend drags the Soldier's body out of sight, Simone takes you out through a back door, across a wide lawn, through a graveyard and into another wood. Pulling you by the arm, she takes you deep into the trees and asks you to crawl into a hole under a tree root. She covers the hole with branches and leaves.

"Don't come out, don't make any sound, until I come for you," Simone says.

She leaves and it is silent. You are terrified but grateful to have found Simone. A long time passes before you hear voices near by.

"Come out now, children!" says a deep voice. You don't think it is the reverend, but you can't be sure. "It's okay," he says. "Come on out. Hurry!"

TO CLIMB OUT OF YOUR HOLE, TURN TO PAGE 73.

TO STAY HIDDEN, TURN TO PAGE 74.

Simone is in danger. You can't just leave her, so you grip the shovel hard and stand your ground. The Soldier closes in, baring his yellow teeth in an evil smile.

"My, what big teeth you've got," you say before swinging the shovel. You hit him in the face, and his smile vanishes.

He pulls his pistol from its holster and points it at you. Feeling like you have nothing to lose, you swing the shovel again, hitting his arm just as he fires. The bullet shatters a window behind you. The pistol drops to the floor.

72

You've never fired a gun before, but it may be your best chance to escape. Can you get to it before the Soldier does? Maybe you should just whack him with the shovel again.

TO REACH FOR THE GUN, TURN TO PAGE 76.

TO HIT HIM WITH THE SHOVEL, TURN TO PAGE 77.

Simone said not to come out until she came for you, but perhaps she sent someone else. You push the branches away and peer around, hoping to see the reverend. Instead you see a Soldier pointing a rifle at you. Behind him stand many others.

"Here's one," the Soldier calls out. "I'd bet everything I have that there are more." He grabs your arm and twists it. The pain bursts through you. He cuffs your wrists together behind your back. It hurts so much you think you might faint.

"They're hiding many children out here." The men clear branches and leaves away from other holes. You lock eyes with another child who's been dragged from her hiding spot. You share a look of terror.

THE END

TO FOLLOW ANOTHER PATH, TURN TO PAGE 9.

Simone said to stay hidden until she came for you, so that's what you do. You hear heavy boots crunching through the forest, and you hold your breath.

Finally the forest is silent again. You keep waiting. Daylight has faded to night by the time Simone shines a lantern above you. "It's okay," she says.

Around you in the forest, you see lots of other children climbing out of holes. Amazing. You had no idea all these hiding places were here.

Simone and the reverend take you and the others into the school. You sit at desks while they bring soup, bread and cheese from a kitchen. You realize you're starving, and you eat greedily.

All the children are housed in a room above the school. Over the next few weeks, Father Michel visits often to teach lessons. Sometimes he tells you stories about his rescue missions. He leaves at night, sneaks through the forest and leads frightened children to safety at his school.

Months go by, and the Soldiers have not come back. You feel restless. You are one of the older children, and you want to help Father Michel on his rescue missions. It would be a way to thank him and Simone and help save other children. When you think of children being hunted by those hairy Soldiers, it gives you the shivers.

On the other hand, perhaps what gives you the shivers is the idea of the Soldiers out there looking for *you*.

TO STAY WITH SIMONE, WHERE YOU FEEL MOST SAFE, TURN TO PAGE 79.

TO ASK FATHER MICHEL IF YOU CAN HELP HIM, TURN TO PAGE 80.

You dive onto the gun and feel its cold steel in your hand for a split second before hearing a loud crack. You touch your head and your hand comes back wet with blood. You realize the crack was the sound of your skull being hit by something. A strange sensation spreads through your body. You look across the floor at the legs of Simone's bed and suddenly feel sleepy and dizzy.

The Soldier pushes you over with his boot, and you roll easily. The gun is no longer in your hand. Did you let it go on purpose? Why did you want it? It's so hard to remember.

As the Soldier picks it up and points it at you, you manage to focus on his face for a second. "My, what big eyes you have," the Soldier says with a snarl as he closes in. Then the world goes black.

THE END

TO FOLLOW ANOTHER PATH, TURN TO PAGE 9.

You can't easily reach the gun. But the Soldier
goes for it. You bring the blade of the shovel
down hard on his forearm, snapping it at an
unnatural angle. The Soldier howls in pain.

A shadow fills the door of the cottage behind
you. You turn to see a tall man in a black robe
standing with a rifle at his shoulder. You shut
your eyes, and the gun goes off. You hear the
Soldier collapse, and his howling stops.

TURN THE PAGE.

When you open your eyes again, the Soldier is lying dead a few centimetres from you.

"I'm Father Michel," the man says.

You spend the next few months living in the school with the other children. You must hide in the woods when Soldiers come looking. But you are never caught. You owe your life to Simone and the reverend, and to your parents, who sent you away to save you.

THE END

TO FOLLOW ANOTHER PATH, TURN TO PAGE 9.

As much as you want to help, it seems too risky. You stay and try to keep your hopes up.

Sometimes Soldiers return to search again. A communication system has been set up in the village to warn Simone when trouble is coming. The children are rushed out to hide in the woods before the Soldiers arrive. You become good friends with another pupil at the school who smiles at you in a way that is different from the others. The smiles make you feel a little less lonely.

When the war ends, you are old enough to start your own family. You marry your smiling friend from school. Many years later, it makes your heart ache with sadness – but also joy – when you watch your own children play hide-and-seek in the woods.

THE END

TO FOLLOW ANOTHER PATH, TURN TO PAGE 9.

Father Michel says he has noticed your courage, skill and desire. He is as grateful for your help as you are for his.

One night he takes you out onto the trail leading back towards your home village. Father Michel has heard that a little girl is fleeing through these woods, just as you did so long ago.

You find the girl alone in the bushes near the same spot where you had hidden from the Soldier in your red cape and hood. Your escape is a distant memory, as though it happened in another lifetime. The wide-eyed girl is trembling. Father Michel reaches a hand out to her, but she turns away. You crouch down to the girl's level.

"This is a good hiding spot," you tell her. "We never would have found you, except that I used it myself once. I hid from one of those mean Soldiers and got away. It seems you and I have something in common – brains."

You talk to the girl for a little while, and gradually she looks into your face. She's still trembling. There's no telling what horror she has seen. But she decides to trust you, and you lead her out of the woods to safety.

Over the next few months, you rescue many more children. You have a couple of close calls, but you are never caught. By the end of the war, you have become a hero to many.

THE END

TO FOLLOW ANOTHER PATH, TURN TO PAGE 9.

CHAPTER 4

Attack plans

You are a special agent working in the Resistance against FocusHood, the corrupt corporation ruling your continent. FocusHood is trying to stamp out all creativity. Creativity leads to inefficiency and to people doing things for fun – or worse, for love – instead of for the State. But creativity, fun and love are things that you believe in. That is why you took the risk of joining the Resistance.

FocusHood started as a software company that designed a program to increase productivity. Soon the company developed a hood that blocked out all distractions. Wearing the hood made people 100 per cent efficient.

Soon FocusHood owned every company on the continent. Every shop, every job, every park, every bit of food was owned by FocusHood – even the government.

Especially the government. The police and trained wolves are now constantly on the lookout for those who don't wear FocusHoods, to force them to do so. You have heard that the hoods will brainwash you into being a slave to the State of FocusHood, which is what your continent is now called.

You are carrying plans, hidden in a cake inside a basket, to Special Agent Grandma (Agent Granny). She's a very important figure in the Resistance. FocusHood would love to imprison her. The information you carry describes an attack plan on one of Focushood's factories. You wear a red cape and hood that is designed to look like a FocusHood but is really just a plain hood.

You were almost through the woods when you heard a voice. Now you hear the voice again: "Where are you going, child?" It is a wolf.

"I am focused on my job," you say, as you have been instructed to do. "I'm delivering this cake to a customer." The wolf looks in the basket, sniffs and strokes his chin. He says you can pass. You walk away, but you feel like you are still being watched. Is the wolf following you? You look back but you see nothing.

Ahead of you the path splits in two directions. The right fork leads to Agent Granny's, and you're in a hurry. But if the wolf follows you, you'll lead him right to her. You're not sure where the left fork goes, but at least taking it won't reveal Agent Granny's location.

TO TAKE THE RIGHT FORK TO AGENT GRANNY'S HOUSE, TURN TO PAGE 86.

TO TAKE THE LEFT FORK, TURN TO PAGE 87.

There isn't any time to spare, so you hurry down the right path, out of the woods, and directly to Agent Granny's.

Agent Granny lives in a plain brown house on a street full of plain brown houses. You know which one is hers because the front door has a tiny red splotch of paint on it – a subtle sign for rebel agents.

When you knock on the door, a voice invites you to come in, but it sounds gravelly. You've never spoken to Agent Granny, so you don't know what she sounds like. If you don't deliver the plans, the attack will probably fail. On the other hand, if a wolf has found her, the plan will definitely fail.

TO WALK IN, TURN TO PAGE 88.

TO LEAVE WITH THE ATTACK PLANS, TURN TO PAGE 90.

You can't risk leading the wolf to Agent Granny's house, so you take the left trail. Through the trees you see more eyes looking at you – more wolves! They're everywhere.

You keep going, turning here and there trying to lose them, but soon *you're* lost. You sit down to catch your breath, and you feel the wolves all around you. Down the path, you see a light. As it bobs closer to you, a human figure takes shape. A headlamp shines from beneath the man's hood. He's carrying an electro-blaster gun.

The wolves retreat deeper into the trees as the man approaches. It is hard to tell the colour of his hood with his light shining on you, but you think it might be red.

"Come with me," he says, kind but urgent.

TO FOLLOW HIM, TURN TO PAGE 91.

TO STAY, TURN TO PAGE 92.

This is no time to be afraid – the Resistance is depending on you. You step inside. Someone in a red hood is sitting on a chair facing away from you. A big, hairy hand holds a thick book.

"Agent Granny," you say nervously. "What big hands you've got."

"The better to work with," the figure says. "And speaking of work, I believe you have something for me," the voice continues.

You're suspicious. "What's the password?" you ask. A low growl comes from under the hood. It makes the hair on your neck stiffen. "That's not the password, Granny."

If it's the wolf, then what has happened to Agent Granny? She's a legendary hero! If the wolf was able to destroy her, there's no telling what he will do to you.

You back up to the door. "Leave the plans, child," rumbles the voice.

TO LEAVE THE PLANS AND RUN FOR YOUR LIFE, TURN TO PAGE 94.

TO TAKE THE PLANS WITH YOU, TURN TO PAGE 96.

It's too risky. You don't trust that the voice was Agent Granny's. You turn and head down the street. There's a café near by where you can hide in the crowd and call Resistance headquarters. Perhaps they've heard something from Agent Granny. You walk through a plaza bustling with people wearing FocusHoods. They are rushing to work with no time to let their minds wander or notice the clouds.

Poor fools, you think. They are like robots. They don't know it, but you're going to save them.

You sit near the back of the café and call headquarters, but nobody answers. A red-caped man across the room catches your eye, but just then a waiter approaches your table. It's a wolf.

"Something to drink?" the wolf asks. Is it the same wolf from the woods? You can't tell.

TO ACT CASUALLY AND ORDER A DRINK, TURN TO PAGE 98.

TO QUICKLY LEAVE THE CAFÉ, TURN TO PAGE 103.

The man knows his way through the woods, and soon you emerge near the edge of town. You walk across a car park towards a petrol station. Inside, the man leads you behind the counter to an office, where another red-caped agent waits.

"I'm Peter," the man says, taking a seat behind the desk. "Agent Granny has been captured by the wolves. By now they probably have her in a FocusHood. She's probably brainwashed and … efficient!" He spits the last word. "Give me the plans," he says, and you hand over the basket. He reaches a finger into the middle of the cake and pulls out a flash drive sealed in cling film.

91

"I'll get these plans to Agent Granny's faction. I need you two to rescue Granny."

TURN TO PAGE 100.

You don't know if you can trust this man. He might be an ally, but the plans you're carrying are too valuable to risk it. "No thank you," you say.

The man grabs your wrist. "Come on!" he says. "Time is short!"

In the woods off the path, a wolf slinks low to the ground, watching, waiting to see what will happen. The man notices too. He tries to grab your basket, but you hold tight. As the wolf approaches, the man takes a step back.

"What's the trouble?" the wolf asks.

"No trouble," the man says. "Just working efficiently."

"Be on your way then," the wolf says to the man. He holds out a paw that suggests you are not free to go.

The man looks at you one last time. "You should have come with me," he says as he walks away.

The wolf takes the basket from your hands and looks inside. "This cake looks very … creative," he says, scraping some icing off with his claw and licking it.

"That is how the customer ordered it," you say.

"Is that right?" the wolf asks. Suddenly he grabs you by the arms and throws you over his shoulder. "We'll just take you in to make sure your FocusHood is working properly."

You are about to be fitted with a real FocusHood **93** and will lose all your creativity and desire for fun. Worse still, the plans hidden inside the cake will be discovered. You have let down the Resistance.

THE END

TO FOLLOW ANOTHER PATH, TURN TO PAGE 9.

You run all the way back to headquarters. All around you, people in FocusHoods are on their way to work, tapping on their devices as they walk. Some are conducting meetings over the phone: "5 per cent." "No deal!" "Deliver by Tuesday!" No making plans for the weekend or discussing last night's TV. Never distracted.

You reach headquarters, hidden in the basement of another brown house, naturally. You use your key card to gain entrance, then head down to the basement hideout. Resistance workers are watching surveillance screens and discussing attack plans.

Your boss, Big Mama, rushes over and hugs you. "What happened?" she asks, looking unhappy. She's holding a device up to her ear, listening to a report.

"What do you mean?" you ask.

"FocusHood wolf agents have intercepted the plans. Were you attacked by a wolf? Are you okay?"

"I left the plans with Agent Granny…" you say. But you realize you made a terrible mistake leaving the plans there. That was no grandma.

Big Mama listens again to the device. "Oh, no," she says. Others in the room stop what they're doing and turn to look. "They've traced the plans to us," Big Mama says. "They're coming."

You hang your red hood in shame. You realize **95** that in order to restore creativity, fun and love, you must first be brave.

THE END

TO FOLLOW ANOTHER PATH, TURN TO PAGE 9.

You tuck the basket under your arm and run. "Come back!" the voice calls after you.

On the street, a wolf slips out from behind a car and starts chasing you, claws clicking on the hard pavement. You dart into a narrow alley where you throw the basket into a rubbish bin and keep running. You'll come back for it later.

When you emerge from the alley on the other side, the wolf is waiting. How did he get there so quickly? Or maybe it's another wolf. They're teaming up!

The second wolf grabs you by the shoulders, and you try to fight him off. You catch a glimpse of the first wolf fishing for the basket in the bin. You're thrown to the ground, and your head is ringing as you see the wolf lean over you with gleaming teeth.

But then you hear a zap, and the wolf collapses next to you.

A tall red-caped man carrying an electro-blaster dashes up. "We have to get that cake back!" he says and runs towards the wolf that is still searching the rubbish. You're not sure you can take any more encounters with teeth and claws.

TO FOLLOW THE MAN WITH THE BLASTER AND FIGHT THE OTHER WOLF FOR THE BASKET, TURN TO PAGE 101.

TO ESCAPE WHILE YOU CAN, TURN TO PAGE 102.

You order a milkshake from the wolf. The man in the red hood sips water and watches you.

When the wolf waiter has gone, you call headquarters again. Big Mama answers. "What's going on?" she asks. "Have you delivered the cake?"

You explain about the wolf's voice at Agent Granny's house.

Big Mama laughs. "No wolf can defeat Agent Granny," she says. "Go back and give her the cake. She's waiting for you."

You leave a few coins on the table and dash out without your drink. As you jog back towards Agent Granny's house, you notice that the caped man from the café is following you. Many people in red hoods are allies – that is a signal to each other. But you can't be sure.

TO GO ON TO AGENT GRANNY'S HOUSE, GO TO PAGE 99.

TO CONFRONT THE MAN, TURN TO PAGE 103.

You ignore the man and continue on to Agent Granny's. When you knock, a raspy voice tells you to come in.

"Now give me the plans," a drooling creature demands as you enter. Big Mama was wrong – it *is* the wolf. You turn to run, but a second wolf stops you. "I've got a nice hood for you," he says.

Later, in a sterile room, you are strapped to a table. A wolf approaches and places a black hood over your head. A feeling you can only describe as electric honey oozes through your brain.

You experience a brief flash of terror as you feel all your human desires well up and then begin to slip away. The wolf watches the screen above you and murmurs, "My, what big dreams you had…"

THE END

TO FOLLOW ANOTHER PATH, TURN TO PAGE 9.

You and a scruffy-faced agent called Dogface Bob sneak on foot towards a prison across town. You have intelligence that Agent Granny is in a holding cell near the gates. Dogface Bob is a highly trained combat soldier. The plan is for him to fight the guards while you cut the power on the electric gates and free Agent Granny.

But as you approach the prison gate, Dogface Bob turns to look at you with cold, yellow eyes. His hood slips down, revealing a hairy neck and long, dripping teeth. A wolf! You turn to run, but he knocks you to the ground. You're taken inside the prison and down a long, cold corridor to a cell where one other person sits alone: Agent Granny.

"Enjoy your last night of free thought, humans," hisses Dogface Bob.

THE END

TO FOLLOW ANOTHER PATH, TURN TO PAGE 9.

The man runs down the alley. You follow. By now the wolf has pulled your basket from the bin and is running in the other direction. The man aims his blaster and shoots. The wolf goes rigid then falls to the ground like a felled tree. The basket clatters onto the street. You grab it.

Later, at a secret base, you and the man deliver the plans to Granny herself, who escaped to safety there. That night you help execute the attack perfectly. You shut down the remote power controls at one of FocusHood's largest factories. Afterwards, as you walk home in the early morning light, you hear something. It's a person whistling a tune. You realize you haven't heard anyone whistle – or sing or laugh – in many months. You smile and whistle too.

THE END

TO FOLLOW ANOTHER PATH, TURN TO PAGE 9.

As the man runs into the alley aiming his blaster at the wolf, you head for the forest. But when you hear another zap, you stop to see what's happened.

A second later the man appears, breathing hard. "The wolf got away with the plans," he yells. Now the Corporation will know what the Resistance is up to."

But you quickly realize that is the least of your worries. Six wolves slip out from between the trees and come towards you. There is no point in resisting.

That night you are fitted with a FocusHood. You feel the needs to love and create evaporate from your heart. In their place is the desire to work. Your first job, fed from the Corporation directly into your brain, is simple: Find Agent Granny and destroy her.

You know you will do it with great efficiency.

THE END

TO FOLLOW ANOTHER PATH, TURN TO PAGE 9.

You glance over your shoulder and see that the red-caped man is right behind you. "Why are you following me?" you ask.

He whispers, "Follow me. I'm here to help you!" You're not sure if you believe him, but you follow him to Granny's hideout. At the door a tall wrinkly woman greets the man, calling him Peter. "This is our new agent," Peter says, gesturing towards you. She reaches for her glasses and asks you for the plans.

Gathering your courage, you ask, "What is the password?"

Granny looks at you, impressed. "Well done," she nods and answers: "Crimson".

The three of you look at the plans while you lick icing off your fingers. Agent Granny makes a few phone calls. The attack is on for tonight.

TURN THE PAGE.

Agent Granny is a wild driver. She careers through the city streets, trying to get to the FocusHood factory in time to drive through the security gate, which Peter will be opening in less than two minutes.

You arrive and see a fire blazing, as planned. You drive right by it and glide through the gate, which lifts just in time. Three other agents tumble out of the van and go on a wolf hunt. It's your job to scale the building and slip into a window on the fourth floor. Once inside, you lock the door to the room and find the main computer server.

But some wolves have found you too. You hear claws scratching at the door and the whimpers of animals desperate for meat.

Quickly you slip a secret flash drive out of your cape. You insert the drive into the computer just as the wolves crash through the door, claws glinting in the soft glow of the computer screens. Instantly there is a popping sound. Lights all over the city flicker, and the wolves drop from their hind legs to all-fours. They look at you with confusion, then slink away, tails between their legs.

The attack was a success! You meet up with the others and return to headquarters. Along the way you see people newly freed from their FocusHoods, looking at the stars in a daze. Four more factory attacks like this and you will have deactivated all the FocusHoods in the State.

But you'll have to be efficient.

THE END

TO FOLLOW ANOTHER PATH, TURN TO PAGE 9.

CHAPTER 5

A little bit of history about Little Red

The story that eventually became "Little Red Riding Hood" was told orally long before anyone wrote it down. Researchers believe that the story may have evolved from a tale told in Europe and the Middle East in the 1st century. This story, "The Wolf and the Kids", featured a nanny goat who warns her kids not to open the door while she is out. A wolf overhears her and tricks the kids into letting him in. He then eats them up.

107

By the 10th century, French peasants were telling a tale closer to the one we know today. A priest wrote it as a poem in Latin in the 11th century, and it spread to Austria and Italy.

The early versions didn't always have a wolf as the villain. Sometimes it was an ogre or a werewolf. The girl did not wear a red riding hood yet. But the main elements – a girl carrying treats to her grandmother and a villain who tricks her – were in place. There was no male adult to help the girl, and she usually escaped on her own.

In the 1600s French author Charles Perrault wrote the first published version of the story. He introduced the red cape and hood and called the girl Little Red Riding Hood. In Perrault's version the girl does not escape – she is eaten by the wolf! In case readers didn't quite understand the meaning of the story, he added a moral to the end: Children should not talk to strangers.

The Brothers Grimm wrote their version of the story in the 1800s. They added the huntsman, who bursts into the cottage and saves Little Red Riding Hood and her grandmother. The brothers even wrote a sequel in which Red and her grandmother fight back. When a wolf tries to trick them again, the grandmother locks the door to keep him out. Then she and Red cook sausages in a pot over a fire. The smell attracts the wolf, who climbs down the chimney and is boiled in the pot.

Today most people are familiar with the Grimms' version of "Little Red Riding Hood". Many creators have fun putting their own spin on it. Author Roald Dahl published a humorous rhyming version in 1982, and Little Red has been retold and adapted in many other modern forms.

An animated film called *Hoodwinked!* was released in 2005. A comical retelling of the tale, the film centres around a police investigation of the Big Bad Wolf's crime.

COMPREHENSION QUESTIONS

⚶ In Chapter 5 the author talks about the "moral" in Charles Perrault's version of "Little Red Riding Hood". What is meant by "the moral of the story"? What is the moral that Perrault's version emphasized?

⚶ This book offers three different stories, all from the perspective of Little Red Riding Hood. How might the stories be different if they were told from the wolf's or villain's point of view?

⚶ Imagine your own Red Riding Hood story. What is the setting? How would the characters and plot be different from the original tale? Would your tale have a moral?

BOOKS

Classic Fairy Tales, Berlie Doherty (Walker Books, 2009)

Grimm Tales: For Young and Old, Philip Pullman (Penguin, 2013)

WEBSITE

www.bbc.co.uk/education/clips/z8wn34j
Watch this video clip to learn about the key elements
found in all fairy tales.